"You are one ugly fish," said Salem. "I'm doing you a favor by eating you."

Salem's friend Roscoe, the greasy alleycat, leaped off the mantel and landed in the aquarium with a splash. This startled the fish. There was a flurry of activity inside the tank, and all the gravel swirled up from the bottom.

For a moment Salem feared the fight would be over before he got into it. He couldn't let Roscoe have all the fun! So the cat vaulted over the side of the aquarium and plunged into the water.

*Time to find the fish and force him to the surface.* Salem saw a mad swirl of bubbles and gravel at the other end of the tank, and he quickly swam over. He expected to see Roscoe chasing the fish, and what he saw surprised him.

The fish was chasing the cat! In fact, he was trying to chomp the cat to bits. Luckily for Roscoe, his fur was so greasy that every bite just slid off. Salem realized that the skinny fish had row after row of sharp white teeth.

*Uh-oh!*

**Sabrina, The Teenage Witch™**
**Salem's Tails™**

Available from MINSTREL Books

# Sabrina The Teenage Witch®

# Salem's Tails®

## GONE FISHIN'

**John Vornholt**

**Based upon the characters in Archie Comics**

**And based upon the television series
Sabrina, The Teenage Witch
Created for television by Nell Scovell
Developed for television by Jonathan Schmock**

**Illustrated by Mark Dubowski**

A
MINSTREL®
BOOK

Published by POCKET BOOKS
New York   London   Toronto   Sydney   Singapore

This book is a work of fiction. Names, characters, places and incidents are products of the author's imagination or are used fictitiously. Any resemblance to actual events or locales or persons living or dead is entirely coincidental.

A MINSTREL PAPERBACK *Original*

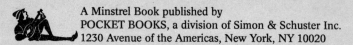

A Minstrel Book published by
POCKET BOOKS, a division of Simon & Schuster Inc.
1230 Avenue of the Americas, New York, NY 10020

Copyright © 2000 by Viacom Productions, Inc. All rights reserved.

Salem Quotes taken from the following episodes:
"What Price Harvey?" written by Frank Conniff
"Disneyworld" written by David Lesser

ISBN: 0-671-03833-8

First Minstrel Books printing January 2000

10  9  8  7  6  5  4  3  2  1

A MINSTREL BOOK and colophon are registered trademarks of
Simon & Schuster Inc.

SABRINA THE TEENAGE WITCH and all related titles, logos
and characters are trademarks of Archie Comics Publications, Inc.

Printed in the U.S.A.

*For Katherine*

Here's Salem, King of the Jungle, out prowling for a
frozen banana. Nothing will stand in my way.

—*Salem*

# GONE FISHIN'

# Chapter 1

The beautiful creature floated through a blue paradise. It had stripes of black and silver, and its tail waved like a silky flag. Salem thought he had never seen anything more beautiful. With its graceful movements, it looked like an angel . . . an angelfish.

The black cat sat on the sidewalk by the window, his tail swishing back and forth. He could spend all day staring at the aquarium inside the fish restaurant.

There was nothing he liked more than watching fish, except for eating fish.

"How can they tempt me like this?" Salem grumbled to himself. "They are almost *asking* me to steal that fish. Or another one that's even bigger."

Of course, the aquarium was supposed to tempt diners to come inside the restaurant. Only the diners were supposed to be people with money in their pockets. Cats were not welcome inside this restaurant, which was a pity. Salem's stomach began to growl.

*No!* That wasn't his stomach growling. It was another cat! Salem turned to see a scrawny gray alleycat standing behind him. The other cat arched his back and hissed at Salem, trying to scare him away.

"Ha!" said the black cat with a laugh. "Napoleon couldn't scare me, and neither will you."

# Gone Fishin'

The gray cat stopped hissing and cocked his head. *Maybe he's never met a talking cat before,* thought Salem. Of course, Salem wasn't really a cat. He was a proud warlock who had been turned into a cat by the Witches' Council. So what if he had tried to take over the world?

Now he lived with a teenage witch named Sabrina and her two aunts. Being a witch's familiar was a dirty job, but somebody had to do it.

"Go away," he told the skinny gray cat. "This is *my* turf. In fact, it's my turf-and-surf dinner."

The other cat began to lick his dirty paw, trying to ignore Salem. Even though Salem wasn't really a cat, he got along okay with other cats. One of his best friends, Lola, he had met outside a sushi restaurant. All cats were united in their love of seafood.

3

Salem turned back to watch the fish in the aquarium, and he licked his whiskers. A waiter walked past with a big plate of fried catfish, and Salem watched him take it to a happy customer. Every person seemed to have a fat fish on his dinner plate. It wasn't fair!

At the back of the restaurant was a big display case full of fresh fish. Salmon, flounder, bass, trout, perch . . . they all looked delicious! Some of those fish were bigger than Salem, and he wondered how he could sneak in there and grab one.

*Hmmmm*, thought Salem. He turned to look at the gray cat, wondering if his fellow feline could be of help. "You look hungry," he said.

"Meow!" agreed the alleycat.

"I'm Salem, and your name is?"

"Rowwrr," answered the cat.

"Roscoe," said Salem with a nod. At least

that's what it sounded like to him. "Okay, Roscoe, here's the plan. We need a diversion, and you will spearhead the attack."

With his claw, Salem drew circles and lines in the dirt. When he was done, it looked like a football play. "These are the tables. You run between them, under them, whatever you have to do. While they're all chasing you, I'll sneak behind the counter and grab a fat salmon. How does that sound?"

"Meee-ow!"

"Good. I'll meet you in the alley."

The door of the restaurant opened as a customer came out. Salem nodded toward the door, and Roscoe slipped inside the restaurant. Salem followed a few steps behind, and he quickly ducked behind a potted plant.

Roscoe knew his stuff. He saw a waiter juggling a tray full of steaming fish, and he dashed between his legs. The waiter screamed with surprise and threw his tray into the air. Dishes, glasses, and silverware came crashing down.

Now everyone watched Roscoe as he darted between the tables. Customers shrieked, and the waiters yelled at him. They chased the gray cat, but they were all a few steps too slow. Roscoe jumped on top of a table and landed in someone's clam chowder. White, sticky soup flew all over the place.

No one was watching Salem as he slipped behind the display case. With his paw, he pushed open the sliding glass door, then he speared a big pink salmon. The fish was so huge that it took Salem all four claws to drag it out of the ice. With a plop the big fish landed on the floor. Ooh, it smelled scaly and delicious!

Salem looked around, worried that he had been seen. But Roscoe was still doing a great job. Two waiters chased him under a table and got tangled up with the tablecloth. When Roscoe clawed their ankles, they knocked over the table and dumped dishes everywhere.

Roscoe grabbed a perch filet off the floor and dashed under a lady's coat. She shrieked, jumped up, and knocked over her table! Then the huge coat began to scoot across the floor with Roscoe underneath it. Waiters grabbed for it, but all they got was a handful of fake fur.

Footsteps thundered past, and Salem saw the cooks rushing out of the kitchen. Everyone was joining in the chase! *This is perfect,* thought the black cat as he dragged his fish through the empty kitchen. Some fresh-baked rolls were cooling on

7

the counter, and they smelled wonderful. Salem grabbed one to go with his dinner.

A few seconds later the cat and his fish were in the alley, hiding behind a garbage can. Salem heard a door slam and more shouting. "You darn cat!" yelled a man. "If you ever come back here again, I'll make cat soup!"

Salem munched on his roll until Roscoe showed up. The gray alleycat was panting and out of breath, but he looked happy. At the sight of the big fish, he licked his whiskers and curled his tail.

"For your bravery, you may have the head!" announced Salem. The gray cat pounced on the fish head and began to eat.

"Roscoe," said Salem, "I think this is the beginning of a beautiful friendship."

# Chapter 2

The next day, two tails swished back and forth under a purple hedge. One tail was black, and the other was gray. Salem and Roscoe were stationed outside the gates of a mansion a few blocks from Sabrina's house. From inside came the cool sounds of a waterfall. It looked shady and peaceful.

"Welcome to my part of town," said Salem. "This is the Hawthorne House, a noted example of neoclassical architec-

ture. It's the biggest house in this part of town, owned by a rich old lady. But we don't care about the house."

Once again Salem started to draw a diagram in the dirt. He drew the walls and the house, then a kidney shape. "This is what we want—the mother lode."

"Rowr?" asked Roscoe.

"A koi pond." Salem licked his whiskers at the thought of big, beautiful carp swimming lazily in a small pond. Some people thought koi looked like giant goldfish, but to Salem they looked like lunch. "I love Japanese food, don't you?"

"Purrr," agreed the skinny gray cat.

Salem went on, "You attack from the east of the pool, and I will attack from the west. We join forces and herd the fish into the north end, where it's shallow. Then we wrestle one of them out of the water."

"Grrr," grumbled Roscoe.

"I know, I don't like to swim, either. Why is it that fish always have to be in the water?"

Just then a gardener walked by with a pair of long hedge clippers. His big feet stopped right in front of them, and his sharp clippers began to cut the hedge. At once the cats dropped their tails. For several moments the man stood above them, clipping and cutting. Finally he moved on, and Salem let out a tense breath.

"The gardeners," whispered Salem. "They're the biggest problem. If they come after you, run for it. It's every cat for himself."

Roscoe nodded. The alleycat's eye twitched for a moment, and he growled. He was ready for action.

"Move out!" This time Salem led the way, with Roscoe slinking along right be-

11

hind him. They slipped through the iron bars on the gate, then scurried across the driveway. Salem headed for the bushes and kept close to the wall, trying to stay undercover.

There were at least two gardeners working in the yard, but it was a huge place. Salem figured they could get in, get their prey, and get out—without being caught.

He followed the sound of the running water, and he found a pile of rocks. His heart thumping with excitement, Salem climbed the rocks to the top. He looked down at a fake waterfall, which tumbled over some reddish boulders into the koi pond.

The pond was a kitty's dream. The shallow water was teaming with fat, spotted fish—yellow, gold, black, and white. Cousins of catfish, the koi had big mouths and long whiskers. Their golden scales glimmered in the sunlight.

Salem heard a sigh, and he turned to see Roscoe grinning like a young kitten.

"I know," said Salem, his voice trembling. "Beautiful, aren't they? I don't see any gardeners around. Are you ready?"

Roscoe was so excited that he leaned too far forward, and his feet skittered on the wet rocks. Without warning, he slid onto his rear end and lunged off the top of the waterfall. With loud yowls, the cat bounced down the rocks, slid across a boulder, and plunged into the water. A big splash scattered the koi in every direction.

Salem scowled. This was not how it was supposed to go! Well, they wanted the fish to be scared, and they were. Roscoe sputtered water and thrashed about, while the koi swarmed around him. Salem figured that he had to save the day.

So he leaped off the waterfall, jumping far enough to get away from the rocks. Still it was a long fall, and the water was icy cold when Salem hit it. He dropped all the way to the bottom of the scummy pond, and he could feel seaweed clawing at his legs.

Eyes wide open, Salem swam desperately to get to the surface. Before he could, a big yellow koi came charging toward him like a great white shark. With its broad snout, it rammed him and drove him farther underwater.

Salem struggled again to get to the surface. This pond was deeper than it looked! Halfway up he felt claws on top of his head, pushing him farther down.

*It's that idiot, Roscoe!* thought Salem.

*He's trying to stand on something, and he picked my head!*

Salem grabbed Roscoe's legs and climbed up his back. Sputtering and gasping, he finally reached the surface. Now it was Salem's turn to stand on top of Roscoe, while he tried to breathe. Without warning, the big yellow koi fish leaped from the water, causing a mighty wave. It washed over Salem and drove him back down into the water.

Now both cats were drowning. Salem saw the big yellow fish cruise past him, and it looked like a life preserver. He reached out with his claws and caught hold of the fish's back. It was like grabbing a torpedo and hanging on.

Salem clung to the koi with all four paws. The koi twisted like a bucking bronco, bouncing Salem up and down as they tore through the water. Finally the

15

koi jumped out of the water, across the pond. Salem knew he should get off, but he was too busy screaming.

The big fish twisted in the air, so that Salem would hit the water first. With a huge splash, cat and fish smashed into the water, and Salem was ripped off his mount. He was still trying to catch his breath when he saw a yellow torpedo headed straight toward him.

"I give up!" he yelled. "I beg for mercy!"

But there was no mercy in the koi's cold eyes. He surged toward Salem like a tiny shark, and the cat swam as fast as he could. Panting for breath, Salem stroked toward the shallow end of the pond.

*I can make it!* thought the cat. *Just a little farther!* Before he could go another inch, the big mouth of the koi closed around his tail. With a jerk Salem felt himself going backward! He tried to paddle with all four feet, but the fish pulled him deeper underwater.

Salem tried to scream, but only bubbles spewed from his mouth. *This crazy fish is trying to drown me!* thought the cat. *I sure hope I have nine lives, because I'm about to lose one of them!*

# Chapter 3

Salem struggled, but a big koi fish had him by the tail. Whipping its sleek body, the koi pulled him deeper into the pond. Other koi fish swarmed around him in a swirl of gold, black, red, and white. They made it even harder for the cat to swim, and some of them bumped him on purpose.

His lungs burned for air, but there wasn't any. Salem slapped his paws over his mouth, but it didn't do any good. He was down to his last breath!

Suddenly a powerful force gripped the scruff of his neck. The cat was jerked upward, with the fish still hanging on to his tail. When Salem broke from the water, all he could do was gasp for breath. He barely noticed the gardener who had saved his life.

Laughing out loud, the man tossed the cat and the fish onto the lawn. Both of them flopped around for a few seconds, gasping for breath.

"I've heard about a drowned cat, but I never thought I'd *see* one," said the man, still laughing.

"I thought I saw another cat run off," said a second voice. "Maybe not. Better put that fish back in the water."

Salem stopped coughing and opened one eye. There were two gardeners, but no Roscoe in sight. Good! His partner

19

had gotten away. One of the men picked up the fish and tossed it back into the pond.

*Hey, they let the fish off scot-free!* thought Salem angrily. *It was mostly the koi's fault, for looking so delicious.*

The first gardener bent down and peered more closely at Salem. "Hey, I think I know this cat." He scratched his hairy chin and nodded. "Yeah, this is the black cat that belongs to the Spellmans. I'd know that ugly puss anywhere."

*Uh-oh!* thought Salem. *I'm busted.*

Sabrina walked in the front door of her house and tossed her schoolbooks on the table. With a big sigh she sank onto a comfortable armchair. It was Thursday—almost the weekend—and she just wanted to relax.

The teenage witch grinned as she

thought about all the fun she would have. Friday night was a date with Harvey, Saturday a party in the Other Realm, and Sunday a date with Harvey. Not only that, but she would earn extra credit in her biology class.

*It's going to be a great weekend. Nothing can go wrong!*

Suddenly Sabrina felt like petting her cute kitty. "Salem!" she called. "Where are you?"

He didn't come running out of the kitchen like he usually did. He didn't come charging down the stairs, either. Where was that cat?

Sabrina heard the closet door shut upstairs, followed by titters of laughter. That must be her aunts, coming home from the Other Realm. Maybe Salem was with them.

Aunt Zelda and Aunt Hilda strolled down the stairs. They were dressed in

fancy cowgirl outfits, with red boots and lots of fringe. Aunt Zelda was thin and stylish, and Aunt Hilda was funny and wild. They were still laughing about something.

Hilda waved her hand with disgust. "When they said it was a dude ranch, I thought there would be some *dudes* there. Not horses! Who wants to meet a horse?"

Zelda laughed, then she noticed her niece sitting in the living room. "Hi, Sabrina. You're home early."

"I've got to rest up," answered the teen. "It's going to be a big weekend."

"Any homework?" asked Hilda.

"No, but that reminds me. I'll get extra credit if I do a favor for my biology teacher. I need you to sign a permission slip." She opened a textbook and took out a sheet of paper.

"Permission for what?" asked Hilda suspiciously.

Sabrina shrugged. "We have some animals in the classroom, and it's my turn to take one of them home for the weekend. I hope I get the tarantula."

"Tarantula?" said Aunt Hilda, making a face. "I don't trust anything with more than four legs." She snapped her fingers, and a quill pen appeared in her hand. With a flourish, Hilda signed the permission slip and handed it back to Sabrina.

"And keep the tarantula away from Salem," said Aunt Zelda. "He'll think it's a cat toy."

"Where is that cat?" asked Sabrina, rising from her chair. As if in answer, the doorbell rang, and Sabrina went to answer it.

In the doorway stood a muscular gardener, holding a wet, miserable cat. "Does this belong to you?"

"Salem!" exclaimed Sabrina with alarm. "Are you all right?"

"He's no worse for wear," said the gardener, handing her the wet cat. "I work for Mrs. Wright, in the big mansion two blocks down the street."

"We know it well," said Aunt Zelda. "How did he come to be there?"

The man scowled. "He was trying to steal fish out of Mrs. Wright's koi pond. He almost got himself drowned. Mrs. Wright says that if he comes back again, she's going to call Animal Control."

"Thank you," said Sabrina, holding Salem tightly. "And thank Mrs. Wright, too."

"Sure thing." On his way out the man added, "If you're going to let him run wild, it might be a good idea to put a collar on him. With a telephone number."

Aunt Zelda crossed her arms and stared gravely at the wet cat. "Oh, we will."

Sabrina shut the front door, then held the cat at arm's length. "Well? What do you have to say for yourself?"

"I'm innocent!" pleaded Salem. "I just wanted to wash my paws, when this big fish jumped out and picked a fight! Who are you going to believe, me or a fish?"

"Salem, you are grounded," declared Aunt Hilda. "And I think the idea of a collar is a very good one."

"With a little bell on it," said Zelda. She pointed her finger, and a bright red collar appeared around Salem's neck. It had a cute little bell and a name tag with the Spellmans' telephone number.

"Oh, no!" groaned Salem. "Now I look

25

like a *teenager!* Maybe I should have my belly button pierced, too."

"I think it's cute," said Sabrina. "Besides, you should be punished. You were trying to catch fish in somebody else's pond? Don't we feed you well enough?"

"In a word, no." With his front paws the cat struggled to push the collar over his head.

"I can make it tighter," warned Aunt Zelda. She leveled her finger at the cat.

"And I can make it pink," said Sabrina.

"No, no!" said Salem quickly. "I'll be good, I promise. I won't take the collar off."

"You had better not," said Sabrina. "Nothing is going to mess up my weekend."

# Chapter 4

On Friday after school Sabrina returned to her biology class. It was her turn to take home one of the class animals for the weekend. She was hoping for the tarantula, or maybe the fat guinea pig.

"Ah, Miss Spellman," said the teacher, Mr. Herbert. "Your houseguest is ready to go."

Sabrina looked hopefully at the tarantula, but Mr. Herbert pointed to the fish tank. Inside the tank was an ugly silver-blue fish with a jutting lower jaw. He wasn't very big, about the size of a man's fist. "You take the piranha."

"The piranha?" asked Sabrina with a shiver. She didn't like the way the fish looked at her.

"Just keep Groucho warm and check the water. Call me if he looks funny. Don't worry about feeding him, because I just fed him."

"Oh, really. What does he eat?"

Mr. Herbert gave her a smile. "Anything he wants. They're meat-eaters, Miss Spellman. Pound for pound, that's the most dangerous creature that lives in the water."

"And the ugliest," added Sabrina.

"Would you rather take the snake?" asked the teacher dryly.

"No thanks!" The teenager grabbed the tank and hurried for the door, struggling with the weight. "Gotta go!"

"Do you want some help?"

"No, that's all right." Grunting, Sabrina pushed open the door. She didn't tell Mr. Herbert that she and the fish were going to disappear as soon as they got away from him.

Before she could do any witchcraft, Sabrina and the fish tank bumped into Harvey. Her handsome boyfriend instantly took over the burden.

"Let me carry that," he insisted. He peered at the ugly fish. "I see you got Groucho. Let me give you a tip—don't use your finger to test the water temperature."

"Thanks," said Sabrina. "I'm looking forward to our date tonight."

"I'll pick you up at six," said Harvey. "It's got to be early so we can wait in line at the concert."

"Okay!" said Sabrina happily. She had

a great boyfriend . . . and a piranha for the weekend.

Salem lay in the crawl space under the house, listening to Sabrina calling him. He wasn't going into the house—he was mad at the witches. It was embarrassing to have to wear a collar with a stupid bell. Every time he moved, the bell rang! He felt like an ice-cream truck.

With this stupid collar, he looked like a house cat. Soon they would make him wear perfume and little bows.

*I'll punish them,* thought Salem. *I'll deprive them of my presence!* He was just doing what all cats do when they get mad—they hide. Cats were masters of the cold shoulder.

Finally Sabrina stopped calling him. He heard her drive off with Harvey. Salem didn't even care if he missed his dinner, he was so mad at Hilda, Zelda, and Sabrina. He was a cat, after all. It was in his nature to be a mighty hunter of lazy fish.

Since it was almost dark, Salem decided it was safe to go outside.

Hoping no one would see him, the cat crawled out of his hiding place. He dashed across the driveway to the bushes, and his stupid bell chimed every step of the way. When he finally stopped moving, it was quiet for a while. Then he heard a wheezing laugh.

Salem whirled around to find his pal, Roscoe, also hiding under the bushes. The alleycat walked over and batted the bell hanging from Salem's new collar. It tinkled merrily, and Roscoe wheezed another laugh.

"Yes, I know it's embarrassing," admitted Salem. "How do you think *I* feel? But

31

I've learned my lesson about fishing. Next time I won't get caught."

"Meow," agreed Roscoe.

"Do you want to come in and look around?" asked Salem. "I've stayed out of sight all day, to make them feel guilty."

Roscoe shrugged and licked his paw.

"Follow me. I know a way to avoid Hilda and Zelda." Salem led the way up the old oak tree which grew by the side of the house. As usual, Sabrina's bedroom window was open, and Salem climbed out to the farthest limb. He leaped easily into the open window. Roscoe was a little scared, but the alleycat also made it through Sabrina's window.

"My witch sleeps here," said Salem, jumping on Sabrina's frilly bed. "I'm her familiar. That's like an assistant who doesn't get paid anything. I tell you, we're treated worse than interns."

Salem led the way out the door and down the stairs. He could hear Zelda and Hilda talking in the kitchen, but no one was in the living room.

Like a good host, Salem pointed out the sights as he strolled around the room. "That's the radiator—a good place to sleep. That's the TV—also a good place to sleep. There are some good dust-bunnies under the couch. That's the fish tank."

Salem stopped suddenly and whirled around. *There was never a fish tank on that table before! What gives?*

Roscoe was staring at the aquarium . . . and a silver fish swimming in it. He wasn't a big fish, kind of skinny, but he was here in Salem's living room. That made him better than a lot of other fish. Both cats swished their tails happily as they watched the new visitor swim around his tank.

"That's what I call room service," said Salem, licking his lips. "Delivered right to my door."

The stupid fish had two cats staring at him, and he didn't look scared at all.

Suddenly the voices got louder. Zelda and Hilda were coming out of the kitchen. Roscoe did a disappearing trick, dashing up the stairs. Salem followed him, and the cats kept running until they reached the safety of Sabrina's room.

Roscoe sat down and pointed to the carpet. Salem knew what he wanted. "No, I won't draw up the plans now," said Salem. "We can't go fishing tonight, because Hilda and Zelda are here. But come back tomorrow night—they'll all be at a party."

Salem gave an evil chuckle. "Nobody will be home but me . . . and the fish. This time there won't be any mistakes."

# Chapter 5

All day Saturday Salem hummed a little song to himself: "Gone fishin', gone fishin', instead of just wishin'."

He was still mad at the witches, so he kept out of sight again. Besides, he didn't want to be caught staring at the fish. Maybe if he pretended not to notice the new aquarium, they wouldn't suspect him when the fish disappeared.

Salem made up a story to tell the witches. He would say that a fishing boat sailed through the house while they were gone. They dropped a net in the aquarium, caught the fish, and went away. *Don't laugh*, thought Salem. *Stranger things have happened in this house.*

The witches were so busy getting ready for the party in the Other Realm that they ignored him. Chattering happily, all three of them vanished into the linen closet. With a flash of light, they were gone. Now he was alone in the house . . . just him and the fish.

He walked through the kitchen and saw a dish of cat food set out for him. *Fools!* He wasn't going to eat that junk food tonight; he was going to eat *fresh fish*. Maybe he and Roscoe would eat the cat food for dessert.

Salem slipped out the back door and waited for his pal to arrive. A little after dark the gray alleycat showed up, looking dirtier than usual. He seemed to be covered in axle grease.

"I'm glad *I* don't have to sleep under cars," said Salem with distaste. "Maybe all that grease will keep you warm when you hit the water. That's what swimmers do when they cross the English Channel."

Roscoe licked his paw and sneezed, making his face look more cockeyed.

"Wait here," said Salem. The cat dashed back into the house. When he came out a minute later, he was wearing a scuba mask and a snorkel. "I want to *see* what I'm doing this time."

Salem began to draw plans in the dirt. "Here's the table and the aquarium. This fish is small compared to that koi we fought—I don't think he'll put up much of a fight. Dive in the tank and force him to the surface. I'll bat him out with my claw. Then it's dinnertime."

"Rowwrrr!" growled Roscoe hungrily.

"Let's go fishin'." Salem led the way into the house and the living room. They circled the aquarium, one cat covered in black grease and another wearing a scuba mask. The fish swam lazily back and forth in the tank. From the corner of his eye, he looked down at them.

"Stupid fish," said Salem with a smirk. "He's not even worried."

Roscoe jumped up on the mantel over the fireplace. He stalked to the end, where he had a perfect diving board to leap into the tank. Salem jumped on the table where the aquarium rested. The fish turned around and swam to the edge of the glass. He looked eye-to-eye at the cat and snapped his jaws.

"You are one ugly fish," said Salem. "I'm doing you a favor by eating you."

Once again Roscoe was overeager. The

greasy alleycat leaped off the mantel and landed in the aquarium with a splash. This startled the fish. There was a flurry of activity inside the tank, and all the gravel swirled up from the bottom.

For a moment Salem feared the fight would be over before he got into it. He couldn't let Roscoe have all the fun! So the cat vaulted over the side of the aquarium and plunged into the water. Unlike the koi pond, this water was nice and warm. Plus he could see perfectly in his scuba mask. *This will be easy!*

*Time to find the fish and force him to the surface.* Salem saw a mad swirl of bubbles and gravel at the other end of the tank, and he quickly swam over. He expected to see Roscoe chasing the fish, and what he saw surprised him.

The fish was chasing the cat! In fact, he was trying to chomp the cat to bits. Luck-

39

ily for Roscoe, his fur was so greasy that every bite just slid off. Salem realized that the skinny fish had row after row of sharp white teeth. In action, his mouth looked like a pair of vise-grips.

*Uh-oh!*

Salem started paddling like a ferry boat, trying to get out of the aquarium. But his actions only stirred up more gravel. In a moment he couldn't see anything at all, but he felt it when he bumped against something cold and scaly.

The cat stopped swimming. Maybe he could play dead! The gravel settled down to the bottom of the tank, and he found himself staring at the fish. Salem wasn't sure if a fish could smile, but this one showed him a lot of sharp teeth.

Salem launched into the backstroke, but the fish attacked swiftly. Jaws wide open, he lunged for the cat's neck.

Salem winced and felt the jaws clamp shut. He was certain his life would be over in seconds.

A moment later he was still alive, but his collar was choking him. He felt himself being dragged deeper into the water. Salem opened his eyes to see that the crazy fish had bitten his new collar!

Now the fish was trying to gnaw through the leather and get to Salem's neck. With all his strength, the cat tried to wriggle out of that collar. If the fish went for any other part of his body, it would be all over!

With a burst of bubbles, Salem pushed the collar over his head and got away. No cat ever swam so fast or leaped so high out of the water. Salem looked like a flying fish as he sailed over the top of the aquarium.

He landed on the carpet, panting for

breath. Roscoe lay right beside him, still shivering in fear. Salem could see bald spots on Roscoe's greasy fur where the fish had bitten him. Those koi had been scary, but this fish was . . . evil!

Salem looked up and saw his new collar floating atop the water in the aquarium. He wheezed a hoarse laugh. "Hey, that collar was good for something after all."

Roscoe spit up some water. He was so weak, he could barely lift his head.

Salem sat up and looked into the tank, trying to find the evil fish. He was lurking near the bottom, as if hoping someone would come to get the collar. "No way am I going back in there," said Salem. "But I'm not done with that fish yet, either."

"Rrrrr," answered Roscoe, sounding just as angry.

"We're going to be in trouble after this,"

grumbled Salem. "We had better lay low for a while. If we slip into the Other Realm, even the witches can't find us."

The soaking cats slunk out the door, leaving Salem's collar floating in the fish tank.

# Chapter 6

Laughing gaily, Sabrina exited from the linen closet. Her aunts were right behind her, and they were all dressed in flowing garden dresses. It had been a grand party, with croquet, Italian ices, and handsome men. Here in the mortal realm, it was past midnight.

"I love seeing handsome males in white tails," said Hilda cheerfully.

"I don't normally like tuxedos," said Sabrina. "But on them, it looked good."

"No, I was talking about the rabbits," said Hilda. "You did notice it was a rabbit show. That was the whole *point*."

Aunt Zelda frowned. "It's surprising how many witches have rabbits for familiars. Rabbits are okay, but they don't have enough personality for me."

Hilda sniffed. "Well, sometimes I think cats have *too much* personality."

Sabrina led the way down the stairs and into the living room. She glanced at the piranha. He was swimming back and forth, as usual. Groucho had a way of swimming that looked like he was pacing, like a tiger in a cage.

"Do you suppose Salem will stay in hiding?" asked Zelda. "Or will he grace us with his presence?"

Something glinted in the fish tank, floating on top of the water. *There shouldn't be any metal in the fish*

45

*tank,* thought Sabrina. She should get it out.

While her aunts complained about Salem, Sabrina walked over to the fish tank and looked inside. She didn't want to just reach into the water, because the piranha looked hungry. So Sabrina leaned over and peered carefully into the tank.

A small red ring floated on top of the water. It looked like a miniature life preserver. The shiny metal was a little bell and a name tag.

"Oh, no!" shrieked Sabrina. She gasped and jumped back from the fish tank. "Not my poor kitty!"

"What is it, honey?" asked Hilda, rushing to her side.

"What happened?" asked Zelda with concern.

With a quivering finger, Sabrina

pointed to the fish tank. She made Salem's collar rise into the air and hover for all to see. Aunt Zelda and Aunt Hilda stared in horror.

"What is *that* doing in there?" demanded Hilda.

Zelda put her hand over her mouth. "Isn't it clear? Salem must have tried to get the piranha and . . . and . . ."

"It ate him," finished Sabrina. "Everything but his collar." Tears welled in her eyes, and her throat felt like she had swallowed a sock. "Wait a minute, there's something else in the tank."

She peered closely at a dark spot on the water, then she wiggled her finger. A clump of wet cat fur rose above the water. It was dark, greasy, and drippy.

"Ewww!" said Hilda. "I don't blame him for not eating the fur."

"Aunt Hilda!" screamed Sabrina. "That's *Salem* we're talking about! All that's left of him is a collar and a hank of hair."

Hilda tried to comfort her. "There, there, honey . . . Salem had a full life. He almost took over the world, twice."

"He knew there were dangers in being turned into a cat," said Zelda. "That's why it's such a serious punishment. Although usually the cat eats the fish, not the other way around."

Sabrina rolled up her sleeves and pointed her finger at the piranha. "You rotten fish! I'm going to turn you into a fish stick!"

Hilda cupped her hand, breaking the spell. "It's not his fault, Sabrina. He's just being . . . a piranha. Besides, you should have warned Salem about this particular fish."

Sabrina flapped her arms in distress. "I know I should have! I kept calling him, but he didn't come. And I got so busy with everything. Oh, we neglected him and left him in danger!"

"Maybe he escaped," said Zelda. She closed her eyes and concentrated for a moment. "No, I don't sense him being in this realm."

"He's gone!" Sabrina broke down, sobbing. The aunts were also morose, and nobody knew what to say.

"We'll have a big memorial service for him," said Aunt Hilda, clapping her hands. "We'll invite all his friends."

Aunt Zelda frowned. "Or at least all his enemies. It should be a big turnout."

Sabrina sniffed, sounding a bit relieved. "A memorial service for Salem? That's so sweet. Will there be a funeral, too?"

Hilda shook her head. "Can't have a funeral. There's no body."

Sabrina started sobbing again, and Zelda scowled at her sister. "Thank you for bringing *that* up."

"Let's get started on the invitations," said Sabrina, trying to be brave. "Do you think he would want a tombstone?"

"There's no grave," said Aunt Zelda. "Where would we put it?"

Sabrina sniffed. "His litter box."

# Chapter 7

After sneaking through the linen closet, Salem and Roscoe were lounging in the sun on a beach in the Other Realm. Well, it wasn't really a beach, more like a tanning salon for familiars. Beside them lay a poodle, a Siamese cat, a rabbit, and a goat, all relaxing. The sand was warm, and the sound of waves crashed soothingly on the stereo system.

A waitress stopped at their lounge

chairs and smiled. "Another shrimp cocktail for you two?"

Salem patted his bulging stomach. "No, I don't think so. How about you, old pal?"

Roscoe burped loudly and shook his head.

"Then I'll bring your bill," said the waitress pleasantly.

"Charge it to the Spellman residence," ordered Salem.

"Rowrrr!" growled Roscoe, not happy about leaving.

"All good things must come to an end," said Salem, slipping out of his chair. "We had better get back to the mortal realm. We have an ugly fish to deal with."

"Meow!" Roscoe's face darkened with anger.

A few minutes later Salem pushed open the door of the linen closet and slipped into the hallway. Roscoe darted after him. At once Salem was on alert—he heard a lot of voices coming from downstairs. Were the Spellmans having a party?

Heavy footsteps thudded on the staircase, and two men climbed swiftly toward them. Roscoe and Salem darted into Sabrina's bedroom and hid behind the door. Watching through a small crack, they saw two men reach the top of the stairs.

"What are you going to say about him?" asked a big man with a ponytail.

The other man was slight and well-dressed. He shook his head. "I don't know. He *was* a snappy dresser."

The two men walked away, speaking in whispers. "Can you believe it?" asked Salem. "That's Drell and the Quizmaster. For witches, this is an A-list party."

Roscoe yawned. He didn't know who Drell and the Quizmaster were, and he didn't care.

"Let's go under the house and spy on them." Salem jumped up on the windowsill and leaped out the window. He landed on a branch and scurried to the ground.

Roscoe wasn't so lucky. He came crashing through the branches and landed at Salem's feet with a thud.

"I'm beginning to see why you aren't a cat burglar," said Salem. "Come on. And try to be quiet."

A minute later they crawled under the floor of the living room and hunkered down in the darkness. Above them was a hubbub of conversation, but it didn't sound very happy. *What kind of party is this?* wondered Salem.

Finally the crowd quieted, and he

heard a voice he recognized. It was Aunt Zelda:

"Thank you, everyone, for coming to this memorial service. What can we say? One of the most famous warlocks of our time has passed away. He was a figure of controversy. He was mean and rotten, but he still left his stamp on both realms."

"Who are they talking about?" asked Salem.

"Although he complained about it," said Zelda, "he accepted his punishment. I think he sort of liked being a cat, and he was a true friend to this family. When you saw him and Sabrina together, you thought maybe Salem Saberhagen could really change. But probably not."

Salem gasped. "They're talking about *me!*"

"Here is Drell to say a few words about our departed friend."

Salem held his breath, wondering what his old enemy would say about him. When Drell was head of the Witches' Council, he led the call to turn Salem into a cat. All that, just for trying to take over the world.

Drell cleared his throat, and his deep voice rumbled. "What can you say about Salem Saberhagen? He was a snappy dresser!"

There was a round of applause, and the Quizmaster shouted, "Hey, I was going to say that!"

Drell chuckled. "Actually it was sort of funny the time he invited the circus into Buckingham Palace. Then when he showed the Chinese how to make fireworks. What about the time we raced the hot-air balloons around the sun!"

The old warlock sighed. "Let's just say

that both realms are duller places without Salem. They're safer places, but duller. He led a wild life as a cat, too. He was always stowing away in Sabrina's backpack and getting himself into trouble. Salem doted on Sabrina—we all know that."

Salem didn't hear what else Drell had to say. He was sniffling too loud. Roscoe let him use his tail as a handkerchief, and he blew his nose into it.

For an hour they listened to various speakers tell funny stories about awful things Salem had done. The final words were left up to Aunt Hilda:

"Salem is gone," she said glumly. "But I know what he would do if he were here. We've got food and drink—let's party!"

Under the house, the black cat wept softly. "Oh, this is so touching! I can't be-

lieve they've gone to this much trouble . . . for *me*."

Roscoe gave a snicker.

"Yes, I know I'm still alive," said Salem. "But I can't spoil this lovely service, can I? When the party gets too loud, they'll have to move to the Other Realm. Then *we'll* have a party—just you, me, and the fish."

The alleycat licked his whiskers and nodded.

Salem and Roscoe stole down the steps into the living room. Behind them, they dragged a bag full of stuff, which clattered across the floor. They didn't really need to be quiet, because the house was deserted.

As Salem predicted, the witches had moved the party to the Other Realm. The only one home was the ugly fish, still swimming around in his tank. Salem looked for party food, but the witches had cleaned up already.

Oh, well, they had food. It was swimming around in the tank on the table. The fish eyed them, then he played like a coy koi. He swam slowly in front of them, trying to look like dinner.

"We know that's an act," said Salem. "Roscoe, begin operations."

At once, the alleycat dragged a tennis racket out of the bag. Then he grabbed several balls of string. *I'm giving up my string collection*, thought Salem, *but it will be worth it*.

Next came pulleys, bits of metal, and the welding torch. The last object in the bag was a baseball glove.

Salem put on his welding mask, making him look like a robot. "Stand back, Roscoe!"

59

When he lit the gas and fired up his torch, Roscoe jumped back ten feet. With sparks flying, Salem bored down on the pieces of metal.

Salem set down his sizzling torch and turned off the gas. Then he took off his welding mask and inspected his master-piece. *It looks like modern sculpture,* thought the cat, *especially with the fish tank.*

A tennis racket extended into the water. The ugly fish swam around the strange object, and once again he seemed to be smiling. The handle of the racket was attached to a metal platform outside the tank. Inside the metal platform was a baseball glove.

Ropes and pulleys ran up to the mantel over the fireplace. They had used those to bring up the platform.

"Roscoe, take your station," ordered Salem. "And no messing up this time."

"Me-ow!" answered Roscoe sharply. The alleycat bounded across the furniture and leaped up on the mantel. He stalked along the wooden platform until he stood right over the fish tank.

Salem took off the welding gear. Swishing his tail, he strolled across the floor and leaped onto the table. Just like yesterday, he went to the tank and pressed his face against the glass. At once the ugly fish swam over to sneer at him.

*Just a little bit more to the right,* thought Salem. He moved to his left, hoping the fish would follow.

*Yes, that's right. Now back up a hair.* Salem sat down. He wanted to look harmless, because he wanted the fish to back up about two inches.

The ugly fish didn't cooperate, so

61

Salem ran toward the aquarium. He hit his head on the glass with a loud "Bonk" and bounced off. The action startled the fish and made him back up a couple of inches.

*Close enough!* thought Salem. He licked his paw, which was the signal.

Suddenly Roscoe dived off the mantel, headed for the aquarium. The fish tensed with excitement, but then he saw that Roscoe was going to miss the water. The fish and the familiar watched the alleycat sail through the air.

The fish never knew what hit him, but it was a tennis racket. Roscoe landed right in the baseball glove, driving the platform down. Like a teeter-totter, the tennis racket shot upward and caught the fish. It shot him out of the water like a tennis ball.

Salem leaped down to the floor and ran

around the table. He found the ugly fish flopping helplessly on the carpet. Now it was Salem's turn to sneer. "Don't ever underestimate a cat."

He heard a skidding sound, and he turned to see Roscoe stop. For several seconds they watched the ugly fish flop around on the floor.

"This is better than TV," said Salem.

Roscoe rubbed his stomach and snapped his claws open.

"You're right," answered Salem. "It's time for the main course. I'll take the tail. You can have the head on this one."

Salem was just about to dig in when a voice called out, "Unpaw that fish!"

He whirled around to see Sabrina staring at him. She was dressed in a black dress, and her eyes were red from crying. It was hard to tell if she was more angry or relieved to see him.

"Oh, hi, Sabrina!" said Salem, backing away. "We were just going to see if . . . if the fish wanted to play cards with us."

"What card game?" asked Sabrina. "Go fish?"

Roscoe instantly dashed for the door. Sabrina wiggled her finger and zapped him back into the room. The stunned cat just sat on the floor and stared at her.

"How did you know we were here?" asked Salem politely.

"I didn't." Sabrina zapped the fish back into the aquarium. The ferocious piranha scooted under a rock and disappeared. "I put a spell on the fish so that nothing else would happen. It notified me when there was trouble."

The teenager stared crossly at Salem. "Do you know that everyone thinks you're *dead?* We had a memorial service, and the party is still going on!"

"Reports of my death were exaggerated," answered Salem.

Sabrina shook her head in amazement. "You were really about to eat that piranha. How did you get it out of the tank?" She looked at the tennis racket in the water. "Wow, that's clever."

"Thank you," answered Salem. "Now can we eat our fish?"

"No! I need that fish for extra credit. Alive." Sabrina frowned, then she picked up her cat and gave him a warm hug. "I should be mad, but I'm just so glad to see you. How about a little tuna fish for you and your friend? From a can."

"Rowrr!" answered Roscoe, jumping to his feet. The alleycat followed them into the kitchen.

"There's something else I want to tell you," said Salem. "You might be getting a bill from the Familiar Fat Farm. It's probably a mistake."

"I bet," answered Sabrina. "Anything else I should know?"

"Yes." Salem snuggled into her shoulder. "I missed you."

Sabrina smiled happily. "I missed you, too."

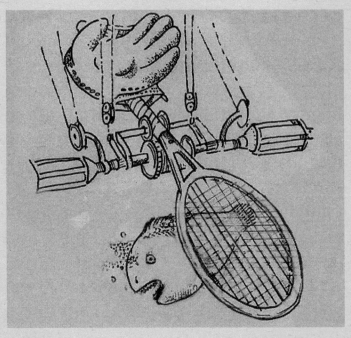

## Cat Care Tips

1. Cats (both female and male) should be neutered around six months of age, but check with your veterinarian. Neutering will help prevent certain diseases such as breast cancer and certain behavioral problems such as urine spraying and aggression toward other cats.

2. Although it is a lot of fun to have a litter of kittens in the house, you must remember that there are thousands of cats who are already in this world who desperately need humans. Please consider adopting a kitten or mature cat from a local shelter. They're listed in the Yellow Pages.

   —Laura E. Smiley, MS, DVM, Dipl. ACVIM
     Gwynedd Veterinary Hospital

*Split-second suspense...*
*Brain-teasing puzzles...*

---

## No case is too tough for the world's greatest teen detective!

# NANCY DREW®

## MYSTERY STORIES

### By Carolyn Keene

*Join Nancy and her friends in*
*thrilling stories of adventure and intrigue*

---

Look for brand-new mysteries
wherever books are sold

---

2313

# Sabrina The Teenage Witch®

# Salem's Tails™

What's it like to be a powerful warlock,
sentenced to one hundred years in a
cat's body for trying to take over the world?
Ask Salem.

**Read all about Salem's magical
adventures in this series based on the hit
ABC-TV show!**

**Look for a new title every other month**

A MINSTREL® BOOK
Published by Pocket Books

2007-10